To those who saw it in me,

Those who believed in me,

Those who taught me love,

And those who held me up.

I dedicate this to you.

CONTENTS

INTRODUCTION

Being in love with someone is a whole new dimension, a whole new experience and a whole new depth of passion. It is an experience that shakes the soul to the core. There is nothing like it and you will not feel as alive before or after the event.

It is magical, it is wonderful, it is beautiful, magnificent and elevating. It is an unworldly experience. You feel high, excited, hyper, as if you are flying amongst the clouds, close to the heavens. You will break your rules for the person, and you will not be ashamed to show it.

The Rhythm of Love aims to enlighten you in the ways of attracting the person you desire, in hope of forming a romantic relationship with them. The winning formula is the effort, time and patience you are willing to invest.

Effort is the blood; sweat and tears you are prepared to shed to do the necessary work in attracting the person you desire.

Time is how long the change you need to undergo will take and what stage of attraction you are in, in the eyes of the person you desire.

Patience is nothing but having confidence in your complete self, no matter what is thrown at you or the challenges you face, even if the results are not clearly visible. You know that eventually you will get what you deserve as a result of your effort and time.

BEFORE WE GET STARTED

The stage of change you are in determines how much devotion you will need. Studies have shown we are only able to retain 7-10% of what we read. Repetition therefore is the mother of invention; the more you read, the more you will remember and the more you will re-program how you feel or think.

If you are new to self-improvement, I recommend that you read the book eight to ten times so that you not only retain the teachings but most importantly, replace doubt and anxiety with self-confidence.

For someone with ample experience, six to eight read-throughs are recommended, and for pros, two to four times will do. Whatever your level, consider this book a companion in your journey.

The journey of love begins.

CHAPTER ONE
THE BEGINNING

THE LOVE STORY

It was the beginning of 2012, and the aftermath of December's bitter cold season lingered.

The noise and blanket warmth of family gatherings had faded into the backdrop, leaving sentiments of uncertainty and downheartedness about the future. Yet another calendar event, the celebration of love, was around the corner. The pressure of it all was too much to bear. Maria had drastically taken a decision: she stood up and marched towards changing her life. In 2012, things had to be different from the previous year. She had arrived over an hour early, eager to snatch a front row seat for better viewing. The hall, with over 800 seats or so, had been empty. She took a seat and patiently waited for the life changing event to begin.

"I couldn't help but notice the contrast of your blonde hair against the red seat," a deep voice whispered behind her.

Maria jumped and gasped for air as she quickly turned behind her.

"Oh, God, you scared the hell out of me!" she said with a startled voice.

"I'm sorry, I didn't mean to scare you," the man replied with a grin on his face. "I saw you as I walked in. I thought, there is someone who I have something in common with," he said as he leaned over. He had strong facial features, the sort that leaves eyeballs staring.

"And what is that?" she asked as she placed her hand on her chest. "Wait, how the hell did you sit behind me so quietly, I didn't hear you walk or anything?" she asked with a squinted face.

"It's rude of me to speak to a lady from behind."

The man took hold of his leather bag, his raincoat and got to his feet. Maria had not yet fully recovered from the fright, and there he was heading her way. "Oh God, why is he coming here?" She quickly fixed her hair and adjusted her skirt.

"May I?" the man asked.

4

"Sure, why not," she replied.

Suddenly a breeze of exquisite aroma swept her senses as the towering figure took a seat beside her.

"Two early arrivers, tells me that we are either eager to start the New Year with some inspiration or we are very punctual people," he said as he stared down at her. His piercing eyes had rendered her speechless for a few seconds. She turned and smiled.

"Why am I smiling at him? This is weird," she thought to herself.

He held his hand near her and said "I'm Bruce. And you are?"

A while later, the auditorium had begun to fill with spectators, the long-awaited event started as the curtains shifted and the lighting dimmed.

Love can be found in the strangest places, when we least expect it. Never lose hope.

CHAPTER TWO
THE RHYTHM OF LOVE

THE LOVE STORY

Maria had met Bruce a couple of weeks before at the motivational event. They spent the entire day talking and laughing, and there was clear chemistry between them both. They could not keep their eyes off each other — well, she could not for the most part. Bruce was tall, dark haired, with gorgeous ocean-like blue eyes. He had a captivating smile, and he seemed successful too. "There was no way he isn't married or with someone," she thought.

At the end of the event, they exchanged numbers and parted ways. Two weeks had past, and he still had not reached out to her. There was not a day that had gone by without a thought of him. Maria grew impatient; she could not bear living in her head anymore. She had decided that she would reach out. It was an uncomfortable decision; her previous lovers were the ones to reach out first. But she really liked Bruce, and she felt something special between them. She romanticised the way, the place and the time they had met.

"Why hasn't he called? Maybe he didn't like me?" she thought. She knew that she could not help but break her rule of first to contact, after all she was 34 now and in need of finding a husband soon. She was ready for change, but how would she go about reaching out? The last thing she wanted was to come across as cheap or desperate.

THE ART OF SEDUCTION

Have you met someone you liked or maybe you have a lost love with whom you would like to rekindle? Do you want to hold the person in your arms, maybe forever? But how do you go about it? The answer is simple: your rhythm of love should be in sync with theirs and then some. Any missteps, any stumble, and any weakness, and they may develop negative feelings towards you. Your approach should be neither too slow nor too fast. Not forced nor careless. The timing should be just right, and it should captivate their minds. "Wow" should be the words that leave their lips.

The rhythm of love consists of six attributes that form the art of seduction. These determine the attraction level the person you desire has towards you.

THE SIX ATTRIBUTES OF SEDUCTION

1. ***Unpredictability*** – your rhythm should be unique so that the person you desire feels a sense of difference every time compared to others who have approached them.

2. ***Challenging*** – your rhythm should demonstrate a sense of self control, leaving the person you desire feeling emotionally provoked.

3.   ***Exciting*** – your rhythm and lifestyle should make them feel a sense of joy, energy and purpose burning within you.

4.   ***Elegant*** – your rhythm should be dignified, graceful and classy in their eyes.

5.   ***Powerful*** – your confident aura should demand attention wherever you go, whatever you do and whenever you speak. It should leave them humbled.

6.   ***Enticing*** – you are able to present a complete package of who you are to persuade them to pursue a romantic relationship with you.

Love has a rhythm; it determines how someone feels about you.
Learn the rhythm and you will win over the love of your dreams.

CHAPTER THREE
THE CHASER

THE LOVE STORY

Maria had finally decided to call Bruce.

"I'll call him after gym in the morning," she thought out loud. "No! What am I thinking? That's way too early! I'll do it after lunch with my girls. No, no, no, it's the weekend, he might be out with his friends. Okay, breathe, breathe."

She took a deep breath in, shut her eyes and gracefully exhaled. "I'll call him after I visit mum and take Pooch for a walk," she thought out loud before pausing. "Oh, God, I need to relax. Just the thought of calling him is driving me nuts. I don't even know the guy, yet I can't get him off my mind. Okay, I need to cool myself off. Cold shower time!"

THE PURSUER

As the pursuer, you possess the powerful ability of being able to change the situation with an element of surprise, while the person you desire has little inspiration or motivation. The change you seek should be unpredictable, challenging, existing, elegant, powerful and enticing. Craft your art of seduction before you make contact and adjust it thereafter to have the desired effect.

Be mindful of the weak position you find yourself in; the powerless and uncomfortable position of the pursuer requires effort, time, patience and the dismissal of your pride. The internal battle of getting the approach right can be daunting and difficult, and it may cause you to sabotage your own success. But if you can reprogram your mind, change your habits, then you can overcome it.

THE DESIRED

The person you desire is in a position of being the decider. They feel a sense of power, control and comfort while you do all the work. Their task is to simply accept or decline. The power, control and comfort leave them in a state of pride. Their pride makes them vulnerable to your changes and surprises. If your seductive rhythm and graceful adjustments are on point, you will be in a position to take their sense of power and control from them, leaving them in a state of discomfort.

A VICTORY OF SEDUCTION

The pursuer's approach should leave the person they desired in a state of discomfort, evoking positive thoughts and emotions, leading the pursuer to appear attractive and valuable.

The art of seduction is your ability to masterfully change roles from being the powerless pursuer to be the powerfully desired.

CHAPTER FOUR

THE MASTERFUL ART OF PURSUING

THE LOVE STORY

A few days later, Maria had yet to make the call.

"What if he is married, and he's in bed with his wife? Oh, God, I'll look like a complete idiot," she thought with a dreadful face. "Actually, I never thought of it," she said delightfully. She quickly jumped up from the sofa. "He might be gay, yeah, that's it. I mistook his charm, his gorgeous face, groomed hair and his broad physic for a man who likes women. Yeah, that's it, maybe he just wanted to be friends," she said as she walked towards the kitchen. She took a sip of a cold drink and continued, "Okay, calling him won't be a problem then. I'll call him, that's right. Maria, you can do this."

A while later, she found herself pacing the living room with her phone clenched in her sweaty hand. She could not do it; she could not muster the courage to.

CONFIDENCE IS KEY

Are you ready to finally contact the one you desire? But your nerves are getting in the way? Are you questioning if you will be able to cope? Will you break down? The fact you have feelings of fear and self-doubt indicates that you are unsure of your approach before you make contact. Remember, any missteps, any stumbles, any annoyance or any sense of weakness will leave a trail of negative feelings towards you. That is the last thing you want. You want positive feelings, so that they want more of you.

To successfully seduce them with positive feelings, you must dive into the mind of the person you desire. Only then, will you be able to remove fear and anxiety from your mind and replace it with confidence in your approach.

THE MIND OF THE ONE YOU DESIRE

To seduce the person you desire, you need to:

1)   Understand how they think and feel.

2)   Use what you have gathered to carefully craft your seductive approach.

The person you desire is naturally in a powerful position as the decider. They feel a sense of control, a sense of choice and a sense of entitlement as a consequence of you pursuing them. Such feelings lend them a sense of comfort.

THE LOVE STORY

Maria finally called Bruce, a week later. "Hello," she said nervously.

"Hey Maria, how are you?" he replied with a joyful tone.

"I'm fine, I've been good, you know," she said with a beaming smile. "I've been so busy; life has been really hectic. I finally found some free time, so I thought I'd call and say hey. I didn't hear from you.

What have you been up to?" she asked. She slapped her forehead — she thought she had said too much.

"I've been good, life is great actually. I've been busy. I am sorry, but I can't talk at the moment," he replied.

"Oh, sorry, we can talk another time," she said with a dejected face.

"I gotta go, we can catch up another time."

"Yes sure, I have some errands to run myself. Anyway. Have a lovely day," she replied, and quickly hung up. "Have a lovely day? What is wrong with me? Why in the world did I even call him? I should have stuck to my rule. Grr, why is dating so hard? I hate myself now," she said with her hands in her hair, grabbing and pulling.

Days later, he never called back. Maria was left feeling horrible. That week she went to work with a sour face.

TAKING THEIR SENSE OF POWER

The feeling of comfort may make the person you pursue careless; they may delay responding to you, they may play cat and mouse games to disrupt your rhythm, they may choose to ignore you or cancel dates. Comfort is not a place you want them to be in or else they will always be in a position of power and control.

How will you know this is the way they feel and think? First, it is safe to assume so since you are the one pursuing and they know it. Secondly, you will know once you make contact.

If Bruce was bothered, he would have called earlier or called back after she called. Even if he was busy, he would have at least shown more interest. Does it mean he dislikes her? No! Does it mean Maria should just move on? No! You cannot give up on getting what you want so easily. She just did not consider his mindset since she was the pursuer. She was already in a powerless position, so why should her approach be the same? By understanding their mindset, you will be able to masterfully navigate around their sense of pride.

Maria calling most likely made Bruce feel proud, powerful and in control. Maybe he was playing the patient game of who is going to break first. He obviously has experience with women. He maybe wants to find out if she can excite him, challenge him, or entice him. Can she be unpredictable? Can she be powerful, leaving him powerless in the process? Do you see the pattern? That is right, it is the rhythm of love. If you seduce the person you desire to want you, to love you, to miss you, then why in the world would they dismiss you?

WHY DO YOU TAKE THEIR SENSE OF POWER?

The reason is that power, control and a sense of comfort makes them feel that they are above you. Since you are the one pursuing, they feel more valuable than you. Pursuing someone is not a crime. It is you going after what you want. But you want to do it the right way; you want them to be in a place where they see you as an equal partner who is equally valuable. If not, why should they notice or be curious about you? Why would they allow thoughts or emotions of you to weaken and control them? Why would they feel for you or want you? Why would they feel the need to pursue you too?

The masterful art of pursuing is to make them see you as a valuable, attractive and desirable proposition.

CHAPTER FIVE

CHANGE AND SURPRISE

THE LOVE STORY

Maria had called back two weeks later. "Hey Maria, how are you?" Bruce asked.

"Hey Bruce, I am good. It's been a while, how are things? I hope you have been fine?" she replied with an excitable tone.

"Things are fine. It's great to hear from you. How's life treating you?" Bruce asked.

Maria got the cue to unleash her master plan, which she had patiently waited on for so long. "I don't know where to begin, so much has happened. The last two weeks have been wonderful, actually the best for a while. We travelled to Italy; Venice was beautiful. Just wow. We ate the most exquisite food." She took a deep breath, sighed and continued, "We then came back, and I finally faced my fears, we went skydiving.

Jumping of a plane is the scariest thing ever. But once we were up in the clouds, it was so beautiful and liberating. You should try it. Oh! Oh, we did some climbing too. Then, I decorated my apartment, it feels like a new place. And I am back in the gym, I feel wonderful."

"Oh, that's great, you sound like you had an amazing time. Who did you go with?" Bruce asked.

Maria took a second or two and then replied, "Hey listen, I am getting a call coming through. I gotta go."

"Oh, that's fine," he replied.

"I'll catch up with you another time," she said before ending the call.

MAKE REAL CHANGES AND SURPRISE THEM

The art of seduction is a back and forth rhythm that blossoms into passion, desire and romance. It is achieved by pulling the person close to you so that you can hold them tight and then you surprise them by pulling away. This time Maria has clearly changed her approach based on Bruce's mind-set from the previous call. She first put in effort by doing things that would transform her mindset, self-belief and confidence. She went out and enjoyed her life. What she said and how she said it; it came from a real place — the depth of her soul. She did not fake it or make it up.

If you fake anything about you or lie, most likely, they will sense something is off. And if they find out, which they will eventually, then why would they stick around? You want them to fall for the real you, not the made up you, so they stay in your arms.

Maria put effort and time into herself, made the necessary real changes and exercised patience, and the result could be clearly heard and felt when she was ready to reach out again. She used her newly found attractive value and surprised him with it. Some might call her approach childish or vengeful, but the truth is, the rhythm of love is unpredictable, challenging, exciting, powerful, elegant, and enticing.

Maria is being unpredictable and challenging whilst she elegantly shares how exciting her life has been. Then she took charge and powerfully left. It was necessary because it is the rhythm that entices Bruce, he does not like the timid and weak kind. She left him feeling surprised with her changed attitude.

Change simply means you adjust and adopt to any situation and any challenges you face. You are able to actualise a better version of yourself in the face of the adversity the person you desire puts in front of you. Your change or self-adjustment leaves them surprised.

Surprise is how you are able to creatively express or showcase your changes through actions. Your proactive actions surprises the person you desire. Surprise could be the things you do or things you say that make them feel positively about you.

The change and surprise approach will leave the one you desire feeling curious. Bruce will be thinking of what Maria is up to. What is she doing? Is she having fun? Does she remember him? Curiosity leads to thoughts and thoughts create emotions.

Emotions create more thoughts, and the vicious cycle of endless thoughts begins. Bruce will be excited to hear from Maria again, because he has been thinking of her.

The aim of taking their power away is to create positive feelings so that the person you desire feels as you do, and they want you as you want them. It should not be used to hurt the person. If you do so, then one day someone will do it to you. Remember, karma has not left this planet.

Once they begin to swim in their own thoughts and emotions, you have begun the process of taking their position of power, control and comfort from them. Again, you only want to do this so that they value you, not to hurt them. And you should stop once they respond to you as a valuable person. Do you think Bruce will be so unappreciative of Maria again when she calls? And when will she call again anyway? He has been thinking about that lately.

The Change and Surprise Strategy is:

1. Your attractive value and uniqueness as a person.

2. The pulling in and pulling away technique.
3. And the use of absences to allow them to miss your presence.

ATTRACTIVE VALUE AND UNIQUENESS

Your attractive value and uniqueness as a person changes how they feel about you, and it keeps them surprised with something new every time you make contact. You are able to transform your essence, leaving them changed and surprised in how they see you. In the second call, Maria sounded bubbly and happy, and she spoke about the things she did. That was her expressing her attractive value as a woman. She was basically saying: you are missing out on all these goodies, come take my arm to find out more.

PULL IN AND PULL AWAY

The rhythm of love is like a seductive dance where the movements consist of pulling the person close to you and pulling away, leaving them feeling emotionally provoked. The back and forth dance determines the depth of affection and desire the person you desire will have towards you.

The Seduction Dance Consists of:

◊ The Pull IN - your rhythm should pull them in with excitement, power and enticement. Anything less would neither leave a lasting impression nor evoke thoughts or emotions.

◊ The Pull Away - your rhythm should pull away with elegance and unpredictability, leaving them feeling challenged. The exit or break should leave them wanting to get close for another dance.

The pull in is the attractive value and uniqueness of you as a person. Maria pulled Bruce in with her exciting lifestyle, her powerful control of the direction of the conversation and her enticing happy and energetic vibe. She did things her way, unapologetically. Bruce was pulled in, she was powerful, in control and she was very comfortable.

The pull away is creating distance or leaving the interaction with elegance, leaving the person feeling intrigued with your unpredictability. Bruce was curious after being pulled in, but Maria pulled away by ending the call when she felt it was right. She became unpredictable and challenging, but she did so in an elegant way.

The purpose of pulling away is not to play wicked games, hurt nor deceive the person; it is to establish attractive value and respect in the eyes of the person you desire. You use the technique when someone dismisses you. Maria surely did not stick around after the second call based on her experience of the first call. Bruce was left feeling that she was neither needy nor desperate. Yes, she wants him, that is why she calls him. But she is not dying for him. That is the impression she left him with.

The pull in and pull away technique begins the cycle of curiosity, thoughts and eventually emotions about you. They will then begin to see you as equally valuable. The pull in leaves them with something to crave, whilst the pull away removes any feelings of neediness that may make them feel more valuable than you. One cannot exist without the other.

ABSENCE TO MISS YOUR PRESENCE

Once you have pulled them in with your attractive value and uniqueness, and you have pulled away, you should utilise radio silence to allow them to assess your attractive value. Radio silence means making no contact. Absence creates curiosity, which in turn turns into thoughts and eventually emotions. If they feel a sense of attraction towards you, they will begin to miss your presence. But you cannot be absent for too long, or the emotions you induced will lose their weight and value. You must pull them back in for another dance sooner rather than later.

Absence while you are in pursuit should be between one to four weeks. Use a shorter timeframe when they are responding to you positively and a longer one if you feel they view you as valueless.

Also, the length of absence should vary between contacts so that you do not become predictable.

Use the absent time to make the necessary changes with yourself so that you are able to surprise them when you make contact.

The dance of love is the pull in to seduce them and the pull away so that they think about of how you made them feel.

CHAPTER SIX
ATTRACTIVE VALUE

THE LOVE STORY

"Hey Maria, how are you?" Bruce asked in his deep and soothing voice. It was a windy weekend afternoon, the cloudy sky obscuring scores of warm rays from reaching the hills of San Francisco. It had been a week since Maria had spoken to Bruce. She had planned her radio silence to be two weeks long before reaching out again, but Bruce had called a week earlier.

"Hey, Bruce, it's nice to hear from you. I'm great, I'm actually heading out to meet my friends; we are off to a weekend trip."

"Oh, wow, you're always doing something. Do you ever have a relaxed weekend, you know, doing nothing?" A tingling sensation shot up from her ears to the back of Maria's head, and it stirred up the biggest grin on her face, stretching from the edges of her lips to corners of her brows.

"Hello, are you there?" Bruce asked.

Not only did Bruce call at a perfect time; he had affirmed her efforts had paid off.

"I am here," she replied as she chuckled. "Life is too short; we only have one. It is for us to make something of it and enjoy it. I don't like sitting around doing nothing. Sorry, I have to get ready, my friends will be here soon," she replied with a mischievous face. She had gotten better at her pull in and pull away strategy, but she had to be careful or she'd over play her hand and leave empty-handed.

"Wow aren't you something. Listen, how's next Saturday for you? I know a great place downtown; they have some of the best food around," he said.

Maria quickly muted her phone. "Yes!" she yelled from the top of her lungs. She hopped on the sofa, thrusting her hands in the air in celebration. "Yes, yes, yes!" she shouted joyously as she jumped up and down on the cushions.

"Hello?" Bruce called out.

"Oh, shit, I nearly forgot about him. Calm down, calm down, Maria! Breathe." She stepped off the sofa, exhaled and unmuted the phone. "Yes, I am here, sorry give me a second, please. I'm doing something."

"Okay, take your time" he replied.

She muted her phone again. "He finally asked me out. Yes!" she shouted, followed by an evil-like laugh. "Okay, calm your ass down, woman, stop acting like a teenager, don't mess things up with your husband to be. Husband? Gosh, just the sound of that makes me excited." She paced around the living room, gathering her thoughts. "I can tell him tomorrow, but I can't cancel my schedule for him, I've been doing so well, all the effort and time it took to get here. I really wanna see him, though, I'm starting to forget his beautiful face, and his smell, ah. Gosh, I'm getting hot now." She sat on her favourite armchair, reclined it back, and continued, "Okay, you've come this far, you can't stop or change your routine. Remember, love is challenging, exciting, powerful, unpredictable, elegant and enticing. Patience,

Maria, patience. If you really want to win him over, you have to be patient. Stick to it until the end."

She sat back up and unmuted the phone. "Hey, sorry about that. I have to go, they are here," she said calmly, "can you call me Thursday evening? I'll give you my availability then." She bit her lip whilst squinting her eyes; they were hard words for her to swallow.

"Sounds like a plan. You have a great time with your friends. Bye for now."

SELF ACTUALISATION

Self-actualisation is realising your full potential as a human-being. Your full potential is the purpose or meaning of your existence. This may be your hobbies, interest, activities or career. A person who realises their full potential will have a sense of fulfilment; fulfilment means satisfaction or happiness within you. A happy and satisfied person is appealing and valuable to the person they desire simply because they have a powerful, exciting and enticing aura surrounding them. People love to be around others who are doing amazing things in their lives, especially if the things they are doing are pleasurable and fun. Who wants to be with someone who is miserable?

In her first call, Maria was in a powerless position as the pursuer, and what made it worse was her inability to express an exciting and enticing purpose to her life. She could not because, up to that point, her life had been plain. But instead of being easily defeated, questioning her self-worth or labelling Bruce, she went out and she got busy on working on herself. She travelled, she faced her fears, she undertook challenging activities, and she worked on being healthy. When she called the second time, the effort and time she devoted to herself paid off. She elegantly expressed her purpose in life, so much so that she had the guts to pull away after she pulled Bruce in. When Bruce called, she made sure, when she got the opportunity, to let Bruce know that she still had purpose in her life. And she stuck to her newly found self-confidence and purpose when she told him to call back to arrange a date.

INTERNAL TRANSFORMATION

Internal transformation is the inner change you undergo as a consequence of self-actualisation.

The transformation has to be real, or else the person will sense it eventually. Pretence or falsehoods may get them to pursue you, but it will not keep them around you. You must therefore clean out all the negative thoughts, experiences and habits, leaving your mind with nothing but positive thoughts. It does not mean that all should be forgotten, it just means that you have transformed into a new you. Internal transformation is taking control of your emotions — your self-control should be effortless.

Remember, the person you desire may employ tactics to test if you are the real deal. These tactics may be designed to make you feel:

Angry – it leaves the person you desire feeling powerful, in control and comfortable. Your attractive value decreases as a consequence of anger. Your internal self-control and presence should be challenging and powerful (two of six attributes of the of seduction).

Needy – it means that you view your happiness and purpose in life as revolving around the person you desire. You need them to exist or to be happy. Neediness sends a message of weakness and low value. Over pursuit can be viewed as being needy. Give them space while you focus on your fulfilment and making necessary changes. Let them know you want them, but you are capable of being self-sufficient.

In her first call, Maria did not let anger or bitterness dismiss or sabotage her chances with Bruce. Instead, she made an effort and she worked on herself. The results were obvious in her second attempt of pursuing Bruce. It left Bruce with a positive lasting impression, so much so that he reached out for the first time. When Bruce called, Maria had the urge to see Bruce the next day, but she resisted her feelings of neediness, and she stuck with being challenging, powerful and unpredictable. She let Bruce know that she was in no rush, making her more attractively valuable in his eyes.

Find your purpose in life and make the necessary changes so that the love of your dreams will find you hard to resist.

CHAPTER SEVEN
THE CONFIDENCE WITHIN

THE LOVE STORY

A year ago, Maria had ended her relationship with Michael. Michael was a successful businessman whom she fell in love with. He had a great sense of humour, and he was a romantic kind of guy. After just six months of dating, he stood on a bended knee and asked to marry her. "I found the most amazing woman in the world, and she means everything to me, and I want to spend the rest of my life with her" were the words that left her in endless tears. Without an ounce of hesitation, she mustered the strength to say, "Yes." He placed the most glamorous engagement ring on her finger. That day was the happiest day of her life.

Her fairy-tale Prince charming and her dazzling diamond ring left all eyes that saw and all ears that heard with envy. Everything in her life had changed from that day, her sleep was deeper, her mood was joyous, her self-care was lengthy and her clothes were stylish. She felt like she was on top of the world.

But it all quickly changed, within a few weeks.

"You never have enough time for us," she always told him. She had not taken Michael's business trips into consideration. Maria sought advice from her friends and family on what she should do.

"I felt that it was too good to be true. Don't you remember what happened to your cousin and how it left her broken?" her aunt Nicole told her.

"Yes, but Michael is different, he is caring, romantic and he loves me," she replied.

"That's what she said. How long have you known him, and do you really know him?" she said with displeased stare. "Look Maria, I really care about you and I don't want heartbreak to destroy you like it did your cousin. He is a man; he is maybe seeing another woman on his business trips."

The thought of it all being a lie had already begun to break Maria. Doubt and fear crept into her life. Nicole advised her to employ clever tactics to force

Michael to give up his business life. She began to dismiss his calls, she became argumentative, she stopped thanking him when he sent her gifts and when they were together, she stopped being loving. She became unappreciative because Nicole's advice was to make him feel worthless, so he would drop everything for her. It was an ultimatum kind of strategy, either her or his career.

"I found someone who really likes me," she once told him over the phone. Nicole had been sitting next to her whispering words in her ears. And so, Michael did as she wanted, and he left his career. She found out that Michael had been telling the truth all along. He had been faithful to her. But a few months later, she ended the relationship. Michael had become a shadow of himself; his attractiveness as a confident man had all but gone. She realised that she had fallen in love with the image and idea of Michael but not Michael the person. Maria also ended her close relationship with her aunt; her vengeful and destructive ways had left a bad taste in her mouth.

Maria spent weeks carrying guilt because of what she did to Michael, and she eventually asked him for his forgiveness. They became friends months later.

WHEN DOUBT AND FEAR GETS A HOLD OF US

Doubt and fear can sometimes deny us the best things in life. When we doubt ourselves, we begin to instil beliefs in our minds that we are unworthy. Unworthiness leads to poor self-esteem, which in turn dents our confidence. We doubt others because we are afraid that we are unworthy, or we fear that the person may be too good to be true. Doubts creep into our mind that they somehow must be deceiving us. We then seek advice from others because we have little confidence in our decision-making, which in turn opens the gates to bad advice.

Maria fell in love with the idea of Michael because of her doubts and fears of her future. She gloated over her engagement to him because it made her feel secure and confident that her life was moving forward. Nicole was consumed by negativity as a consequence of insecurities, and she either had no good faith in others or she intentionally sabotaged her niece's relationship. Michael placed his confidence in his career; it gave him a sense of control, comfort and power, but as soon as he gave it up out of fear of losing Maria, his self-worth and confidence diminished. Doubt and fear, as a consequence of bad experiences or lack of emotional growth, can become and define us, unless we begin to have confidence in ourselves.

TWO FORMS OF CONFIDENCE

Have you ever met someone who is not attractive, yet they are so confident? The person may be over overweight, yet they are dating someone very attractive and slim. This is because they have realised the true source of confidence.

There are two sources of confidence: the spiritual source and the superficial source.

Spiritual Confidence comes from within your

soul. People who are naturally spiritual or who have undergone spiritual awakening, tend to rely on their natural source of confidence. Their confidence does not rely on external factors, making it generally constant. If external circumstances in their life changes, their natural source of confidence puts up a barrier.

Superficial confidence comes from external factors. These factors may be appearance, social status or material possession. People who rely on these unnatural sources find themselves having confidence that fluctuates regularly. If their unnatural source of confidence runs dry, self-doubt and fear take hold of them.

The mistake most make is believing that real confidence comes from our appearance, our status in life or wealth. These may give a sense of false confidence because without them you would not have a sense of self-worth. Have you ever come across a person who is so good looking or someone who is wealthy, but yet they are so shy, withdrawn, angry or hostile in crowds? This is because their source of confidence comes from an unnatural place. However, superficial confidence has its benefits; it allows us to reap the rewards of our hard work and as human beings we thrive on admiration as a consequence of what we have attained.

THE GIFT FROM WITHIN

There are some who seem to have all the confidence in the world but, yet the one they loved left them. The reason is most likely that their superficial confidence easily attracts the person they desire but overtime it is unable to keep them around. There are plenty of men or women who have left a physically attractive or wealthy lover for this very reason. The major problem with superficial confidence is the source that it derives from. People who rely on their superficial source usually do not devote effort, time and patience on self-improvement. Why should they? They have gotten used to getting what they want with their appearance, status or wealth. So why should they put in so much effort becoming better internally?

Overtime they become predictable, unchallenging, unexciting, inelegant, powerless and they cease to entice their lover to remain in their arms. Their lovers may stick around hoping for change, but the question is, will they accept change? Because superficial confidence is easily plagued with self-doubt and fear, especially when external circumstances change, the person reacts to demands of change from their lover in a predictable, unchallenging, boring or powerless way.

Michael left his career as soon as Maria threatened him; if he was well read in the art of seduction, he could have responded and solved the issue without giving up his career. You should not rely on superficial confidence, because if the one you desire runs into your arms, but they later discover that you easily crumble in the face of challenges, then their attraction towards you will begin to dwindle.

Spiritual confidence allows you to face the challenges life throws at you. The reason the overweight guy is appealing to the attractive slim woman and why she sticks around is because his source of confidence is constant in the face of adversity. It allows him to showcase himself as being worthy and valuable.

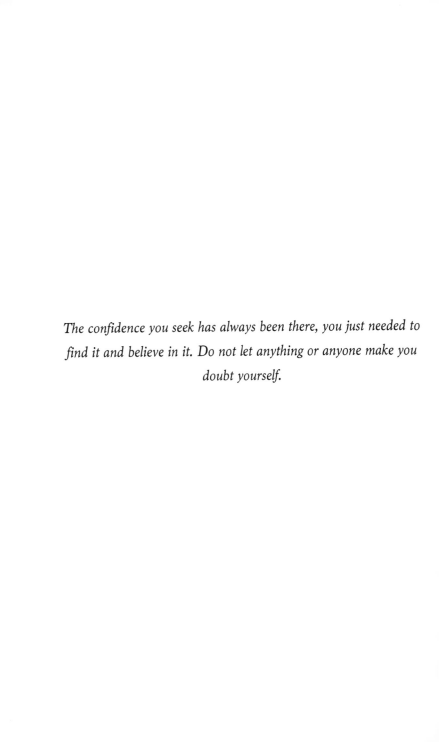

The confidence you seek has always been there, you just needed to find it and believe in it. Do not let anything or anyone make you doubt yourself.

CHAPTER EIGHT
PRACTICE TO BE CONFIDENT

THE LOVE STORY

"Hey Maria, what's up?" Bruce said. He had called her around 8 p.m. on Thursday evening. The night sky was shimmering in the moonlight with stars visible in the backdrop of blackness. Maria had been anticipating Bruce's call since the beginning of the week. In fact, since she had arrived in her two-bedroom apartment, she had been waiting for his call. The call was brief; Bruce arranged to pick up Maria on Saturday evening, at 8 p.m. sharp.

Maria took the longest bath that evening; she could not help but grace every room in her apartment with her love songs. Before bedtime, she practiced her positive affirmation. She had been doing so for a number of weeks now, and her self-belief had changed because she had reprogrammed her mind with positive thoughts about herself. She vowed to never let fear or doubt, or anybody's advice, influence her life.

YOUR SPIRIT

Your spirit encapsulates your entire existence, an existence brought to life so that you can contribute to the universe. Your purpose on earth makes you as valuable as the soil that gives life to acres of green fields, the sun that brings warmth or the rocks that hold everything together. You are special in your own kind of way. We all are. To find the confidence from within you, you need to dig deep and evaluate yourself as a human being. You need to find your true value — the positives and dreadful negatives.

Once you do so, you will discover that:

1. You are not as valueless as you led yourself to believe.
2. The negatives are not as bad as you or others made you believe, and they can be worked on.

3. There is more value or talent left in you that you have yet to discover.

THE LIST OF NEGATIVES

Before we begin practicing in believing in you, you need to write a list of all your doubts and fears, from childhood to adulthood. All negative thoughts that you think about yourself or that others have said about you. Try to keep each of the negatives to a maximum of three words.

Before calling Bruce the second time, Maria began the process of self-evaluation and self-discovery. She started with a list of all her negative thoughts.

I'm bossy	I'm scared
I'm possessive	I'm difficult
I'm easily influenced	I'm argumentative
I'm alone	I'm easily angered
I'm getting old	

THE SOURCE OF NEGATIVES

Once you have written down the negatives, you could spend some time evaluating the source of each of them. Writing is therapeutic, it is liberating, it is eye opening, and it sets you free.

Maria found the following sources:

I'm possessive – she's possessive because she has a low self-esteem. She feels she is not good enough, so she is afraid of losing the person to someone better than she is.

I'm bossy – she is bossy because she likes things to go her way. She has gotten her way since she was young, as her dad spoilt her. If things do not go her way, she is afraid that she may lose control.

Easy influenced – she is easy influenced because she has little self-confidence. She is afraid that her way ruins things, so she asks and takes advice from friends or family.

I'm alone – fear of being alone makes her feel sad and fearful of the future. She stays up at night crying sometimes.

Not good enough – she feels she is not good enough because of past failed relationships.

I'm difficult – she says she is difficult because she is afraid of being heartbroken again.

I'm argumentative – she argues because being made to feel wrong makes her feel insecure and worthless. She likes things to go her way, even when she is wrong, it just feels better. She avoids any discussion that makes her feel bad.

I'm easily angered – she gets angered easily when she is afraid, when she's insecure, when she feels she is losing control or things do not go her way.

The common source of Marias negatives is fear of her perceived worth, fear of losing control, fear of being hurt, fear of being made to feel worthless and fear of trusting her judgement along with a few bad habits she picked up when she was young. These fears cause her to have self-doubt, which makes her bury her self-confidence in a mountain of negative thoughts. That mountain of negativity becomes her.

THE LIST OF POSITIVES

Write a list of positive things about you. They have to be things about your personality or internal attributes, including all the positive thoughts that you think about yourself or that others have said about you. Try to keep the positives to a maximum of three words. Maria wrote her list.

I'm funny	I'm giving
I'm loving & caring	I'm adventurous
I'm thoughtful	I'm open minded
I'm creative	I'm loyal & honest
I'm loved & cherished	I'm playful
I'm social & fun	I'm trustworthy
I'm hard working	

POSITIVE AFFIRMATION

Affirmation is a technique where you read out true statements about yourself with confidence. These true statements are positive things you worked hard to list. A daily routine of reading out the value you bring to the universe will replace the negative thoughts with positive or amazing things about you. The idea is to reprogram your mind so that it changes the way it thinks.

AFFIRMATION SCHEDULE

The next step is to create your schedule of reading out your positive attributes based on your confidence level. For each you read out, you should spend five minutes reading the list of how amazing you are over and over again.

CONFIDENCE EXERCISE

The level of your confidence:

⇒ Low Confidence – you should read out loud your positive list three times a day for five minutes. That is five minutes in the morning, five minutes midday and five minutes before bedtime.

⇒ Medium Confidence – you read your positive list twice a day, in the morning and before bedtime.

⇒ High Confidence – you read your positive list once a week, maybe at the beginning of the week. It is just to maintain your level of confidence. Once you feel that your confidence level has increased, you move on to the next level. If it decreases, you move back down a level to increase your routine of affirmation.

To uncover your inner confidence, you need to devote effort, time and patience in your daily routine of positive affirmations. The more you practice, the more confident you will become.

CHAPTER NINE
PERSONAL & PRIVACY

THE LOVE STORY

Maria finished work early on a Friday afternoon, and Michelle had come to pick her up. "So, the date is on for tomorrow? Finally! I'm excited for you, I hope he is the one," Michelle said with a hint of sarcasm. Maria had known Michelle for 18 years, to be exact, and they were inseparable best friends.

"I have a feeling he is the one, since we met there hasn't been a day, I haven't thought about him," Maria replied.

"Didn't you say the same about Michael?"

Maria was seated on the passenger side of Michelle's convertible. She gazed at her with a stern stare. "Did you have to bring him up?"

Michelle chuckled, "I'm just saying you don't know Bruce well enough and you haven't dated him yet."

"And how long did you know Derek for? It took you two damn years to realise he wasn't the one?" Maria replied harshly.

Michelle had been single for six months—the longest she had ever been.

"Okay, I get your point, you're right. I knew all along that Derek wasn't the one, but you know me, I hate being alone. Plus, I hate the thought of sleeping around. But I am learning how to be alone now, it's hard. I'm 36, will I ever find true love?" Michelle replied with tears falling down her cheeks.

Maria sighed and reached over, lending her hand for Michelle to hold. "I know it is, but it's for the best. Have you started reading the book I gave you, The Rhythm of Love?"

"No, I haven't yet," Michelle replied while wiping tears from eyes.

Maria held Michelle's hand tightly, rubbing her shoulder to comfort her. "You have to, it is life changing. Look at me, have you ever seen me this confident? And

Bruce is pursuing me now. It teaches you to find yourself, so the one for you finds you."

The two had arrived at their destination, and Joanne, Susan, Megan and Diane were waiting inside the bar. Maria had later found out that the others had known about Bruce and her date with him tomorrow. She asked Michelle to accompany her to the toilet.

"Why did you tell them about Bruce?" Maria asked angrily.

"I only told Diane, seems like she can't keep her mouth shut. I'm sorry, she just asked if you were seeing someone, and I briefly told her that you met someone."

KEEP YOUR CARDS CLOSE TO YOUR CHEST

When you are pursuing the person you desire, it is important to keep your cards close to your chest. If you choose to reveal your cards to friends, family or associates, then you must know the flaws of human nature. Even the closest friends or family are capable of negative emotions that may lead them to:

1. Gossip – people generally love something to talk about. The more thoughts, feelings and secrets you reveal, the more gossip will prevail.

2. Feel Jealous – jealousy is a negative emotion felt by someone who desires you. Your friends or associates may view you as the person they desire. If you reveal information about the person you desire, they may feel jealous and act negatively or gossip.

3. Feel Envious – envy is wanting something that somebody else has or wants. Your friends, family or associates may want the person you desire for themselves if you reveal details about them.

4. Be Spiteful – spite is having malicious intent to cause harm to someone. Anybody you know, including family, may seek to sabotage you pursing or having a relationship with the person you desire.

Because human beings struggle with controlling their emotions, and we are unable to decipher someone's true intention, it is best to keep your cards close to your chest when it comes to your love life. Anything you reveal may sabotage your success with happiness.

BAD ADVICE

We are unable to differentiate good advice from bad advice we receive from family, friends and associates because of lack of experience or we doubt our own decision making. Low self-esteem causes you to have no confidence in yourself. Before you take advice from anyone, you should:

1) Question the motive of the person giving the advice. Are they influenced by negative emotions stated above?

2) Assess the positive and negative consequence of the advice. Will the advice increase or decrease your attractive value with the person you desire?

To evaluate if the any advice will have a positive impact or improve your chances, you should always rely on the six attributes of the rhythm of love. Will the advice be challenging, unpredictable, exciting, elegant, powerful, and enticing? Bad advice results in the opposite effect of the six attributes.

Do not allow others to dip their hands in your love affair. If you do, they may run off with your honey.

CHAPTER TEN
THE FIRST DATE

THE LOVE STORY

The day had finally arrived, it had been three months since Maria had met Bruce at an improbable place. There he was, outside her street. Maria had been peeking through the window of her apartment. She had stood by the window for the past fifteen minutes. She quickly shut the curtains, dashed to the other side of the living room to switch on the lights. "This dress won't do for him." She hurried to her bedroom, undressed and slid into a white dress with a blueish flower-like design that stretched from the left side of her shoulder to her right knee. The dress accentuated Maria's fine shoulders, long lean arms and slender figure. She wore white matching heels with a blue bow tied in a knot on top.

The evening had been warm, the perfect ambience for the long-awaited date. "Oh my god, my heart is pounding so hard," she said with her hand placed against her chest. The doorbell rang, and Maria exited her bedroom, stopping near the door frame to gain her footing. "My knees are weak; the way this is going I'll be on the floor." She stood straight, took a big breath in and thought. "Get yourself together, Maria, you've been waiting for this day for so long." She gathered strength and walked down the staircase to the front door. A gush of a familiar scent graced her nostrils as the door swung open. Bruce stood tall, at 6 feet and 2 inches, with a beaming smile. He wore a brown jacket with a blue shirt, black pants and black shoes.

"Hello Maria," he said as he smiled. "These are for you."

"Stay calm," she thought with a smile stretching across her face. "They are lovely, thank you. I'll take them up, just a moment." She climbed up, passed through the hallway to the dining where she placed the bouquet of a dozen flowers on the table. Bruce offered his arm as she returned.

"Where are we going?"

"We are going somewhere special," he replied.

She turned and glanced at him. He had seated himself behind the driver's side.

"Don't get too excited Maria. Remember: be challenging, unpredictable and powerful."

His presence was overwhelming; quiet at times. He seemed to be in deep thought as he stared out of the car window.

The car had been parked at the front door of a tall skyscraper. Maria walked over to the entrance. "I always thought this was some kind of a business building. There is a restaurant here?" The entrance had been laced with red carpet leading up some steps.

"They serve some of the best food in the country here," he replied as he offered his hand.

They boarded the lift to the top floor of the sixty-story building. Bruce held the door for Maria as she entered. The restaurant had tables covered with the most exquisite tablecloth, and the finest glass and silverware. "Wow, this place is lovely." Bruce held the chair for her, and she took a seat.

"I would have thought a restaurant like this would be packed," she said.

Bruce had been staring at her, his cheek resting on his palm, his elbow placed on the table.

"Is this how...," she began before biting her tongue. "I shouldn't mention other women," she thought, "It's weak and insecure. That's the old me. Believe you deserve the best, because you do." She glanced at the menu, redirecting her mind away from the noise in her head.

"Are you not having anything to drink?" she asked, as she lowered the menu.

"I am; I'm having what you're having."

"What if I get something you dislike?"

"I am sure you're worthy of suffering for."

Maria's face lit up; she quickly lowered her eyes back to the menu. "I am sure that's what he says to all women."

Bruce was charming and handsome. His unyielding confidence added to his aura. "I'd better rise to the occasion, no more doubt or fears." The main course had finally arrived.

"Bon appetite Ma'am," the waiter said.

"Sir, if there is anything else, please don't hesitate to ring the bell."

"I think the place is too quiet."

"Ah, yes. Right away." The waiter sounded two claps, and the place was filled with some soothing classical sounds. Maria grabbed the cotton cloth and placed it on her lap. "He is smooth, very smooth, I'll give him that."

Beyond the glass walls of the place, the city lights offered the backdrop with the most magnificent picturesque view. The setting was perfect. She could neither have dreamt for a better date nor envisioned herself with a more fascinating man. A man of few words but when he spoke, his words mattered.

"I've told you a lot about myself. Tell me little about you?" Maria asked.

"The night is long, I am of less importance for now," he replied. Bruce was attentive to who she was as a woman. It made her feel special, like she mattered. She grinned each time she revealed herself to him. The laughter's came naturally, too.

By the time dessert had been served, the butterflies had taken hold of her. The giggles, the stares, and the twiddling with her hair, they all became more frequent.

"What am I doing? I'm behaving like a teenager. If this goes on any longer, I might as well make out with him right here." She gently wiped her mouth and fixed her hair as she stood on her feet.

"Excuse me, I have to use the toilet," she said before walking off.

"Sure."

"How is the date going?" Michelle asked.

"It's going great. He is so calm, and his vibe is so damn sexy. He is charming too, and so attentive. He's just amazing."

"I'm so happy for you and jealous at the same time. What will you do?"

"I've got to stop getting too excited and regain control. I need to read my list of positives quickly. I got to go now. Call you later. Love you."

A short while later, she had returned. "It's getting late; I have an early start tomorrow," she said with a stern face

"That is fine, we'll be on our way." Bruce followed Maria to the elevator.

"Why is it taking so long?" She had pressed the button numerous times. The relaxed atmosphere had clearly changed, to a tense one. The elevator arrived and she hurried in. Bruce followed right behind her.

"Why are you mad at me?" He had gotten close as she turned, staring right in her eye. She panicked and stepped back onto the wall. He moved up-close and placed his hands against the walls, trapping her in-between.

"I asked you a question. Are you avoiding me?" He leaned his face right up-close to hers.

"No, I am not," she replied, staring right at his lips.

"Then what is it?"

"I don't..." She was lost for words.

For the first time in her life she felt like she never felt before. The feeling that touches one's soul. It was surreal.

It was a once in a lifetime kind of an experience. She would not miss it for the world.

She reached forward and touched his lips with hers. The softness, the warmth, and tenderness; it made her feel alive. The lift fell back down sixty levels. Sixty levels of the most passionate kisses that graced her body, mind and soul.

He dropped her off back home, and they parted ways with memories worth cherishing for days to come.

CHAPTER EVELEN
THE ART OF MESSAGING

THE LOVE STORY

It was late afternoon; Maria had been lounging on the sofa talking to Michelle on the phone. Suddenly, her phone vibrated; she had received a WhatsApp message from Bruce.

The message read: *"Hey Maria, hope you had a great start of the week. You came to mind today."*

"Michelle, he's just texted me," Maria said excitedly.

"See, you were worrying for nothing."

"I know the date was three days ago, but it felt like forever. Let me call you back, I need to spend some time working on my reply."

"Oh, what will you say?" Michelle asked.

"I don't know yet, maybe I'll tell him to come over now and I'll be waiting for him in the shower. Just the thought of it excites me," she replied laughing. "Anyway, I gotta go."

Maria wrote her first draft of the WhatsApp message, it read: *"Hey Bruce, so happy you messaged me, haven't been able to get you off my mind. Since the date, I have been thinking of you. The week has been great, how has yours been? xxx"*

She took some time to assess the message. "The first part of the message I am pouring my heart out. Come on, how is that challenging? I'm handing myself on a plate," she thought.

Her second draft read: *"Hey Bruce, my week has been great, how has yours been? Xxx"*

"Argh, it's not exciting, no details of what I have been doing. Also, the question at the end will lead to endless back and forth messaging, nothing to entice or challenge him. I want another date; the end has to be powerful and unpredictable," she thought.

The third draft read: *"Hey Bruce, I had a lovely and busy week. Apart from hectic work, I've been attending my cross-fit sessions, they've been amazing. I'm learning to cook some new dishes, too, thanks to a book my friend gave me. Anyway, looking forward to seeing you soon."*

"Now it's exciting, enticing and unpredictable, but the ending is kind of eager and needy. I can't say that yet, we just went out three days ago. It's not unpredictable and challenging. I need to end it with something that is a pull away, so he becomes curious and wants more."

The fourth draft read: *"Hey Bruce, I had a lovely and busy week. Apart from work, I've been attending my cross-fit sessions, they've been amazing. I'm learning to cook some new dishes, too, thanks to a book my friend gave me. Speak soon."*

"Speak soon? That's kind of harsh. It's like my intention was to gloat and close the door in his face. Also, I didn't ask anything about his week. It's not elegant at all, it's plain rude and selfish."

The fifth draft read: *"Hey Bruce, I had a lovely and busy week. Apart from hectic work, I've been attending my cross-fit sessions, they've been amazing. I'm learning to cook some new dishes, too, thanks to a book my friend gave me. Hope you had a lovely week too. Glad to hear from you."*

"Ahh, much better. Glad to hear from you entices him to message back without making it obvious that I want him to. Now that's challenging, unpredictable and powerful. I've pulled him in, and I'm pulling away with elegance," she thought. She took an hour to compose her reply message, and then she took another 30 minutes to make sure it was perfect before sending it.

THE RIGHT WAY TO MESSAGE

Every interaction you encounter with the person you desire is an opportunity to showcase your attractive value and to seduce them to want you.

The right way to message consists of:

1.   Your actions before you receive the message.

2.   Composing the message.

3.   Timing your response.

4.　　　Your actions after you send the message.

BEFORE YOU RECEIVE THE MESSAGE

Messaging apps such as WhatsApp, Facebook Messenger and others, display your online activities. If you were online regularly and then you received a message from them, they could make assumptions, based on your past daily activity, that you were ignoring or avoiding them if you suddenly disappeared for a few hours.

Your actions before you receive a message will determine how they view or feel about you after they have sent you the message. You will find it difficult to be challenging, unpredictable and to be powerful if they figured out your movements before you even make them.

Maria changed her online presence before Bruce had sent her the message. She would go online once in the morning, and once in the afternoon. She informed her girlfriends and family she would only respond to texts immediately, otherwise they would have to wait. Bruce would have been unable to figure out her activity.

Her mysterious aura led him to be curious, which made him to have thoughts of Maria.

COMPOSING THE MESSAGE

When you are composing a message, you should utilise the six attributes of seduction to construct a perfect message so that you leave the person you desire feeling positively about you. The general rule of thumb is that at least two thirds of the message should be about your attractive value and the rest should be a statement, asking or answering a question.

Maria pulled Bruce in with her attractive value, as most of the message was about things she did. Then at the end, she pulled away elegantly without seeming to be disinterested or shutting him down.

TIMING YOUR RESPONSE

The time it takes to respond is important in maintaining or increasing your attractive value. Immediate responses leave the person you desire feeling powerful, in control and comfortable while at the same time lowering your

value. Taking too long to respond may make it seem you are not so keen to communicate with the person you desire. The timing has to be just right. The time it takes to respond changes as your relationship progresses from a first few contacts, to the dating stage and to having a long-term relationship.

For early contact after meeting, the response time should be two to four hours. After the first few dates, the response time should be one to two hours. At the early stages of a relationship, the response time should be thirty minutes to an hour.

Remember, love has a rhythm. The time you take allows you keep the flames of attraction alive.

AFTER YOU SEND THE MESSAGE

Your online presence after you send the message determines how you affect the person you desire. If your online presence is frequent, and they respond immediately, they would expect you do so too. Therefore, it is important that after you send the message, you come off online and follow a strict timetable to when you will log back in. The strict timetable should be consistent throughout the week. This will allow you to have a powerful impact when you do respond, it would leave the person you desire feeling challenged by your unpredictable response time. We want them to feel that you are valuable and make them curious about you.

Maria responds to Bruce either early morning, and late in afternoon. She follows a strict timetable so that Bruce is unable to predict her movements. Once she does respond, she would wait till the next planned time to go online. Again, she interacts with family and friends via text or email because these platforms do not display her online presence.

The art of messaging is the vibe you give off before you compose your wonderful piece and after you have signed, sealed and delivered it with love.

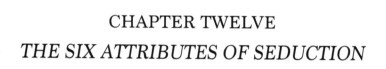

CHAPTER TWELVE

THE SIX ATTRIBUTES OF SEDUCTION

THE WAY OF SEDUCTION

The six attributes of the rhythm of love are the guiding force in the art of seduction. The attraction level towards you is determined by these six attributes. They should be used in all forms of contact, whether it is direct or indirect contact.

FORMS OF CONTACT

There are two forms of contact, direct contact and indirect contact. The person you desire will be observing whether your direct or indirect contact will increase their attraction level towards you. The six attributes will determine how they view and feel about you.

Direct Contact is when you approach the person you desire by making contact. They include face to face, voice call, video call, messaging, email or letter.

Indirect Contact is when the person you desire is observing you without making contact or sometimes without you being aware. These include watching you at the same place of location or social media stalking.

THE ATTRIBUTES IN DEPTH

1. Unpredictable – your actions should be unique so that the person you desire feels a sense of difference compared to others who have approached them.

   ◊ Direct Contact – your direct contact should be unpredictable based on how you view the person you desire. If they are the type of person who feels powerful, in control and comfortable, then you should change your approach and surprise them unpredictability.

   ◊ Indirect Contact – your presence in the same place or location should surprise them with

◊ changes that you have made. Your social media should also be unpredictable and varying. It should be about who you are as person, your attractive value.

2. Challenging – you are challenging by demonstrating a sense of control, leaving the person you desire feeling emotionally provoked.

◊ Direct Contact – your contact should be challenging by having control of your emotions, thoughts and body language. If your emotions, thoughts or your body language reveals how you feel so easily, you will not be a challenge to figure out. Without curiosity, there is little thought which means less likelihood of attraction developing towards you. If you are not a challenging person, you may easily hand over power, control and comfort which may reduce your attractive value.

◊ Indirect Contact – if you will be at the same location, by chance or on purpose, your body language should be a challenge to read.

Your social media presence should not reveal your feelings or state of mind towards them. Make sure that you have a happy and healthy lifestyle image on display so that when they stalk you, they see you as attractively challenging because your happiness is not dependent on them.

3. Exciting – your direct or indirect presence should make them feel the flames of joy, energy and purpose burning within you.

◊ Direct Contact – your approach should showcase that you have a healthy lifestyle with purpose and fulfilment. Your tone of voice, dress sense, your body language and how you express yourself should demonstrate a sense of excitement for life. An exciting person will have a higher attraction value than someone who is not.

◊ Indirect Contact – your presence in a particular place or social media should showcase your excitement for life.

4. Elegant – your direct or indirect presence should be commanding, graceful and classy in their eyes.

   ◊ Direct Contact – your approach should be elegant when you pull them in and when you pull away. You do so in a respectful, mature and dignified way. The opposite of elegance is being rude, dismissive or disrespectful in the way you pull them in and the way you pull away. Being disrespectful reduces your attraction level.

   ◊ Indirect Contact – your approach should be elegant in the way you interact with others, because the one you desire will be observing to see if you have a cheap or crass attitude.

5. Powerful - your direct and indirect approach should demand attention with your confident aura, wherever you go, whatever you do and whenever you speak. It should leave them humbled.

   ◊ Direct Contact – your approach should demonstrate confidence by approaching them with bravery in how you empress yourself in your voice or body language.

The opposite of powerful is fearful, doubtful, submissiveness and neediness. Confidence is your ability to control negative emotions or thoughts and being brave despite the challenge.

◊ Indirect Contact – your approach should showcase your confidence wherever you are and wherever you go. This includes all places you grace with your presence, including social media.

6. Enticing – your direct and indirect approach presents a complete package of yourself to persuade them to pursue a romantic relationship with you.

◊ Direct Contact – your approach should deliver your complete package; it should include the other five attributes. The more you present to the person you desire, the more likely you will increase your attractive value. If you present two attributes, you will need another encounter to present the others to ensure you leave them with a lasting impression. If you do not get the chance to, then you will have wasted your opportunity.

◊ Indirect Contact – your indirect approach should demonstrate your complete package in various places and on social media.

CHAPTER THIRTEEN

THE MAGIC OF FALLING IN LOVE

THE LOVE STORY

"I really enjoyed tonight," Maria said. She had been standing on the landing of the steps to her apartment. "It's too soon to ask him in. Even if I want to, I shouldn't. If only he knew how powerless he makes me feel," she thought. It was another Saturday evening; a week had passed since their first date. Bruce had called Maria a few days prior. To Maria's surprise, things had moved swiftly. Her rhythm of love had worked its charm. He could not get her off his mind. He stood on the sidewalk, looking up toward her. They had returned from a theme park.

"Oh, God, what is he doing?" she thought nervously. Bruce had placed his foot on the step. He wore a raincoat, where his hands had been tucked, and a hat casting shadow on his face.

"It's getting late," she said with a hasty tone.

Hushed and unhurriedly, he ascended the stairs. "He's coming up. What should I do? I need an exit plan quickly." She inhaled a deep breath, giving air to her throbbing heart. With barely enough time to gather her thoughts, his towering frame was already standing near her. "What should I do? I feel like running inside and shutting the door behind me." Her knees had been trembling. She took a step back. "I am a grown ass woman. I got this. Don't do anything silly, you don't wanna lose him." It was nearly midnight. The landing was poorly lit. A gash of wind had whizzed by, shifting her dazzling green dress along. Bruce moved to her side to shield her against the breeze, whilst she pressed her dress against her thigh.

"I think it's getting late," she muttered. She kept facing straight down the stairs, keeping her eyes away from him. He drew his hand from his pocket, laid hold of her chin and turned her face towards him.

"It'll only take few minutes," he said with a rich and soothing voice. She could not help but turn her slender figure toward him.

"His voice. And that smell, it always gets me,"

she thought as she faced his chest. His lengthy raincoat wrapping around her as it flapped. The trees planted along the sidewalk hissed and rattled with the wind. The neighbouring apartments and passing vehicles added to the vibrant atmosphere. She placed her hand against his chest, lowered her eyelids, inhaled a deep breath and soaked up the moment. Bruce moved her face upward. She could barely see his piercing eyes amidst the shadow. "He makes me feel so at peace and powerless. I've never felt like this before," she thought. He shifted her hair behind her ear and gently caressed her cheek.

"What are you doing?" she asked.

"I am admiring how beautiful you are." He then held her chin as he reached down with his lips. The first kiss was brief. A peck that had lasted a few seconds. He pulled back and stared right at her. Her eyes had adjusted, and his eyes overwhelmed her. It was as if she had known him in another life. "I think I have really found him." He reached down for a second kiss, and it felt like an eternity. It was if time stood still. Passing cars had frozen, the trees had been stiffened, and the noise from the apartments muted. The passion, the chemistry and the rush that she felt was magical and sensual. She placed both of her hands on his cheeks and held him for a little while before breaking free.

"I'm sorry, I have to go; I have to use the toilet. I'm sorry," she said with an unsettled face. She turned toward the front door of her apartment, dug in her bag and laid hold of her keys. "Oh, God, why is my hand shaking so much?" She quickly opened the door, turned back and said, "I'm sorry I'll call you." She fought the urge of wanting to slam the door shut. "Oh, God, I can't be around him anymore," she said as she leaned against the door. Maria slid down and sat on the floor. "I think I'm in love. It's too soon." She sat still, trembling and in awe of what had just happened. Half an hour later, she still had not got herself together.

A week later, Maria was in her apartment. She had returned from work. It was a Friday afternoon; the sun was setting beyond the horizon of the apartment balcony window. She threw her briefcase on the coffee table and sat on the sofa. "The week has been so long.

Worst one in a while. Things had been going fine. I haven't heard from him since. I hope he isn't upset that I walked away from him," she thought as she untied her shoes. "I will call him or else he'll think I don't care." She laid flat on her back, staring at the ceiling. "Why am I feeling guilty? I am worth the challenge. He has to see me as valuable. Maybe the way I walked away wasn't elegant, but I couldn't help it. I would have been all over him." She sat up and continued, "I think it's time. I'll invite him over for dinner."

Sunday evening arrived. The buzzer to her door had rung. Maria wore a cream silk dress hanging by a thin thread on her shoulders. The round table stood beside the balcony, set with candles, wine and the flowers he had given her.

"Hey, glad to see you," she said as he opened the door. Bruce leaned forward and gave her a peck on the cheek.

"Glad to see you, too." Bruce climbed the stairs behind her, with his eyes fixed on her hourglass-like figure. Maria had let down her hair; she was bubbly, playful and seductive.

He sat at the table as she served dinner. He was as attentive to her as he had been on the first date. She found it hard to resist his charm.

"When was your last relationship?" she asked.

"Well, a gentleman doesn't tell."

"Oh, come on, it is not fair, I tell you everything." She had reached over and struck him on the shoulder.

"That hurt, careful or you'll send me to hospital," he said smiling.

"Whatever!" She sipped on some wine while she scanned his broad shoulders, muscly arms and soft lips. Bruce wore a burgundy coloured polo-shirt and some denim jeans. "He hasn't looked at them even once. Doesn't he like them? Maybe they are not big enough?" she wondered as she placed her hand on her cleavage. The dress revealed a fair display of her bosom.

"So, are you going to tell me?" she asked.

"Oh, you mean if I have dated a woman as beautiful as you?"

"You know what I mean," she said with a stern look. She raised her glass; and took another sip while fluttering her eyelashes.

"Well, probably never. None of them compare to you." He looked at her dead in the eyes. A surge of excitement, from the pit of her belly to the private places, stirred her desire. The response caught her off guard. The tension between them began to build. Maria flicked her hair as she stood on her feet.

"I made a lovely dessert. Let me get it. By the way, what music are you into?"

"Any, as long as it's not too wild." Bruce stood up and continued, "I'll help you clear the table." Maria walked over to her living room, and she filled her home with some soulful music.

"I'll be right back," she said. She spent some precious time pampering herself. When she opened the door, Bruce stood outside her bathroom.

"Oh, God. You scared me," she said as she struck him on his broad chest. "What are you doing?" He moved towards her, grabbed her by the cheeks and passionately kissed her. She stood powerless, surprised and frozen. But then, excitement came to her again, intensified tenfold. Maria hopped on his waist and wrapped her legs around him.

"Where is your bedroom?"

"I think we are moving too fast," she replied as she stroked his hair. Bruce moved towards the wall, and he kissed her again. The passion, and the chemistry between them was off the charts.

"Does this feel too fast for you? Tell me and I'll make my way home," he said as he gasped for air. She was sweating and breathing heavily too.

"Why would you want to go?" she asked.

"Because I want you. Are you not my woman?" He had said the right words. Maybe a little too soon, but, the right ones, nonetheless. She felt the same, she was his and he hers. "It's that way." She pointed. "Through the first door to your left." Bruce laid her on her queen size bed. They undressed each other, pausing in between each effort. The breaths became heavier, and the clothes fell on the floor. The long-awaited day had finally arrived. Bruce made love to her, like she had never felt before. All through the night, till the break of dawn. It was worth the wait. She laid on his chest, as they slept through the morning.

CHAPTER FOURTEEN
GETTING AN EX BACK

THE LOVE STORY

It has been six months since the first date. Bruce and Maria have been an inseparable item. They spend most of the weekend together; Maria would stay over at Bruce's place and he would stay over at her apartment.

She had fallen deeply in love with Bruce. She had found the one for her, her knight in shining armour. Not an hour went by without her thinking or daydreaming about the time she spent with Bruce. Wherever she went, she would have Bruce in her thoughts. She would message Bruce in the morning, and afternoon and call him in the evening. He would reciprocate by reaching out to her, too.

As time went by Maria lessened her attention on things that gave her fulfilment and purpose in life. Her hobbies, interests and activities took backstage. She found little joy in them. They did not compare to what mattered to her the most. She devoted most of her free time to Bruce. After all, he was now the source of her happiness.

The inevitable day finally came, on the 20th of November 2012. "I think we need a break," Bruce said as he broke the news to her. The words plagued her mind for weeks to come. The breakup occurred after six months of togetherness. Maria tried everything to get him back. She begged and pleaded. She tried to reason with him. She sent him heartfelt messages. And she even tried the mutual friend's route to vouch for her. Nothing worked. Maria was left devastated and heartbroken. She called in sick for work. She spent Christmas alone. Her messy house, the darkness and the comfort of her bed became her companion.

The year had come to end, and though it had started as a gift from the heavens, a wish from the stars, it ended as the last one did. On New Year's Day, Bruce was tagged with someone else in pictures. He seemed happy. He was accompanied by a gorgeous girl with hazel eyes and black hair. She sat on his lap while kissing him on the cheek. It was the final curtain call for Maria. All hope was lost.

LOVE WITHOUT A RHYTHM

The art of seduction ignites the flames of love in the person you desire. The positive emotions you induce cause them to want you. Love without a rhythm is like fire without the fuel that keeps it burning and alive. The fuel of love is the six attributes of seduction. They ignite and keep the passion of love alive.

Maria had forgotten that love has a rhythm. She felt that once she had gotten together with Bruce that just being with him was enough. She stopped doing things that had made her attractive and valuable in the first place - the things that made Bruce want her. In doing so, she became needy, which made her predictable, unchallenging, unexciting, powerless, and inelegant. She stopped enticing him with who she is as woman. The person that he came to love and admire. There was nothing left for Bruce to hold on to.

MAINTAINING YOUR ATTRACTIVE VALUE

Once we are in a relationship, we develop a sense of ownership and comfort. We forget the reason the person chose to be in a romantic relationship.

To maintain your attractive value, you must:

- Focus on things that give you a sense of fulfilment and purpose.
- Utilise the six attributes of seduction to keep the passion of love burning.
- Use the change and surprise strategy to breath excitement and unpredictable into the relationship.

HOW TO GET AN EX BACK

Getting the one you love back means starting afresh, leaving the history you both had locked in a box of the past. Before you initiate contact there must be sufficient space so that any negative feelings or perception of you is replaced with positive memories. Time is your friend, so you must exercise patience and put in the necessary effort to rebuild your attractive value and self-confidence.

Take a few weeks to undertake the necessary changes so that you surprise them when you do make contact. But be mindful that they may be doubtful and may not be receptive. Nonetheless, maintain your goal of rebuilding your image and taking their sense of power away slowly but surely until you induce curiosity, and you ignite the feelings that they once had.

The wealth of knowledge in this book will be your guide in regaining the flames you once had with them. Read repeatedly as advised so that you will have the necessary tools to win back the love of your dreams.

142

THE LOVE STORY

"I had made a mistake and you should give us another chance. I have grown and I want us to work," she said. She had called Michael. He gave thought to her proposition and they got back together weeks later.

On July the 19th, the day she had dreamed of had finally arrived. Maria walked down the aisle with her father on her arm. Michael had a beaming smile as he watched his bride stand beside him. The pastor read the vows and asked, "If any of you have a reason why these two should not be married, speak now or forever hold your peace." The hall had been packed with a few hundred guests. Michelle and the other girls had been present.

Suddenly, the enormous doors swung open, letting rays of light in. "I do!" Bruce yelled. Maria turned towards the exist in shock. She felt a rush that brought back the memories along with the emotions that came with it. "Not again," Michael thought. Maria glanced at

Michael, and then back at Bruce. In her mind, she had let Bruce go, but her heart never did. She lifted her long wedding dress and she turned towards the aisle she'd walked down.

Bruce smiled as she ran towards him. He lent his hand and gave her the warmest hug. Michelle stood up and yelled, "Yes!' The spectators stared with sickened faces.

"I know I never said these words to you, but I love you and I always will."

Maria wiped a tear drop from her face and replied, "I thought I'd lost you forever." She leaned over, and they touched lips for the first time in a long while. The two left in a hurry and drove off into the sunset.

True love does not die, no matter how long time has passed. Finding the one for you is a journey worth taking. You only have one life; live it, experience it and explore it to the fullest.

To Be Continued.

Printed in Great Britain
by Amazon

49542826R00095